THERE'S A
FROG
IN MY
SLEEPING BAG

THERE'S A FROG IN MY SLEEPING BAG

SUSAN CLYMER

ILLUSTRATED BY PAUL CASALE

A
LITTLE APPLE
PAPERBACK

SCHOLASTIC INC.
New York Toronto London Auckland Sydney

ISBN 0-590-88026-8

12 11 10 9 8 7 6 5   8 9/9 0 1 2/0

Printed in the U.S.A.   40

First Scholastic printing, March 1997

To my mother,
Susannah Dorothea Keyt Clymer,
who raised me with
a sense of wonder

Contents

1
Farewell!

Janna slipped her blue and gold pencil out of the sharpener and blew on the point. She didn't really care about sharpening her pencil. She was here to spy! Her pencil with the school colors had shrunk from full size to only three inches long in the last few minutes. Janna stood on her tiptoes again to look out the classroom window.

This time she saw a big yellow school bus turning into the parking lot. "The bus is here!" she sang out.

Students tumbled out of their seats and hurried to the window to watch the bus pull up. Even the kids taking Mr. Jenkins's last-minute math quiz dropped their pencils and followed.

The teacher ran his fingers through his hair, frowning at Janna. That's when she remembered that he had asked for *Sixty Silent Seconds*.

Janna tossed her ponytail over her shoulder and gave the teacher her oops-I-made-a-mistake grin. She didn't wait to see Mr. Jenkins's reaction before she turned back to the window.

"Oh, boy! Oh, boy! *Oh, boy!*" David exclaimed, pushing in to stand next to her. "Three whole days at camp!"

"Outdoor education center," Micah corrected, straightening his glasses. "We'll be learning about nature for fifty-four hours."

Janna rolled her eyes. She didn't care what her best friend, Elizabeth, said, she still thought Micah was a strange guy.

Why, he'd worn his favorite long-sleeved *white* shirt for their first day of camp!

Elizabeth scooted in under Janna's arm to be in front, but that was no problem. Elizabeth was almost a head shorter. "Look!" Janna cried, pointing. "Our bus driver has a mustache!"

"Maybe he's a magician and will make the bus fly to camp," David answered.

That made Janna giggle, and then all the other kids surrounding her. David laughed, too, bouncing up and down on his toes. Standing still was not David's strong point, but he did have the best imagination in the class.

"Organize your desks, Camp Kids. Then head out to the bus!" Mr. Jenkins called. "Your parents are waiting to say good-bye."

Chairs scraped and desktops slammed.

Elizabeth fed their class hamster, Squeaks, an extra handful of sunflower seeds.

Micah lifted the lid off the spider cage and stroked their pet tarantula with one finger. "Good-bye, Hairy," he said. "See you in three days."

As Janna trooped out of the room, her stomach suddenly flip-flopped, like a pancake being tossed in the air. She took her time spreading a towel along the bottom of the door so Squeaks couldn't escape while they were gone.

Next, Janna stopped in the hallway to get a drink . . . a long drink.

Janna was the last one out the back door of the school. She saw Mrs. Grand, the custodian, throwing suitcases and duffel bags into the back of the bus. The other third-grade teacher had gotten sick, so Mrs. Grand, who was Micah's Aunt Grace, had offered to go along to take care of the girls. As usual, Mrs. Grand wore a bandana tied around her neck. Her bandana today was covered with pictures of little campfires.

That's all Janna got to see before her father and little brother, Manuel, surrounded her with hugs. "Good-bye, sweetheart!" her father exclaimed, crouching down to give her a big squeeze.

"Please don't embarrass me," she whispered, but her arms sneaked around her father's neck to hug him back. Her throat had a lump in it . . . a growing lump. She couldn't make herself release her father. Janna leaned into his chest, smelling his shaving cream like she used to when she was younger. To her amazement, her mind started screaming, *No, no! Don't let me go!*

She couldn't be afraid of a little thing like going away to camp, could she?

"I'll miss you, *hermana*!" Manuel cried, then burst into tears. *Hermana* means "sister" in Spanish.

Janna looked around wildly. No one else was crying . . . just a member of her family. She pushed away from her dad. Janna patted her brother on the head and raced to the bus.

"Have a good time!" her father called.

Janna slid into the seat next to Elizabeth. As the bus doors closed, she peered out the window. Her brother was clutching Dad's knee and yowling at the top of his lungs about not wanting his sister to leave. At least most of her classmates couldn't understand him, since he was wailing in Spanish.

How mortifying! Janna stared down at her hands in her lap as the bus pulled out of the parking lot. Yet she could barely swallow past the now giant lump in her throat. Goose bumps rose on her arms as Martin Luther King Jr. Elementary vanished in the distance. To Janna's surprise, she had to clamp her mouth shut to keep herself from yelling out, "Stop the bus!"

2
The Hidden Candy

Janna dragged her trunk two steps closer to the cabin. How ridiculous that she was supposed to do this herself! Anna bounced past with a pack on her back and a sleeping bag under one arm. Janna sighed. Perhaps she shouldn't have packed so much.

At least she could see her cabin now. The sign on the front said RED FOX. Each cabin was named after an animal that lived in Kansas. What seemed like a lifetime later, she dragged her trunk through the doorway.

Janna hesitated. Oh, no, her worst fears were coming true! This cabin was much too small for ten girls. The bunk beds had skinny little mattresses. There weren't even any rugs on the floor. Well, that was all right. She'd brought her own pink rug from the bathroom at home. Mama would probably be missing it about now.

A soft red ball sailed across the room above Janna's head. Sidney knelt on her top bunk and caught the ball with a cheer. Then she tossed the ball back across the room to Anna. The rest of the girls chattered and giggled.

"Over here!" Elizabeth called, waving. She sat cross-legged on her bed with her flashlight in her hands. She had saved the top bed in her bunk for Janna.

Janna tossed her mermaid sleeping bag up on the mattress above her head. Then she climbed up to arrange her pillows and set out her stuffed animals — her leopard named Leppi, and her frog named Ribbit. She tucked her long stuffed snake all the way around the edges of her bed so it would surround her when she slept.

That made her think of her real animals. How could her pets survive without her? Janna's chest ached with worry. Would Mama remember to give Cheeser, the hamster, her daily piece of cheese? Cheeser was one of Squeaks' babies that had been born last fall in Mr. Jenkins's desk drawer.

Would Mama give Trashtruck his special treat? The cat used to live out by the Dumpster at school until Janna had given him a home. Yesterday, Janna had made Trashtruck a peanut butter and sardine sandwich for a treat.

Swallowing, Janna slipped Ribbit inside her sweatshirt for company. She'd spent the night at Elizabeth's, but other than that she'd never been away from home. Janna peered over the edge of her bed down at Elizabeth's bunk. Her best friend's book lay next to her pillow, and a tiny gray stuffed seal slept on the book.

Sidney, on the top bunk beside Janna, had tacked a picture of her family up on the wall. The owl sitting on her pillow looked real. Did all the girls have stuffed animals? Anna had a teddy bear.

"I like your snake," Sidney said.

Janna picked up the snake's head. "Thankssssss," she replied, pretending to be the snake. "My name is Ssslithers. Don't worry, I don't eat owlssssss. Too much sssstuffing."

Suddenly Elizabeth leaped off her bed and hurried toward the far window. "I saw something move in the woods!" she cried, pointing. The other girls crowded around her.

All except for Janna. This was the private moment she'd been hoping would happen . . . a time for her secret! Janna sneaked a cloth sack out of her lace pillowcase. Last night, she'd printed BRUSH BAG along the side of it in big black letters. Janna hung the little purple bag from a hook on the wall by her pillow.

Actually, it was her Life Savers bag. Janna had no idea how anyone in their right mind could expect her to do without Life Savers for three whole days.

Oh, she knew she wasn't supposed to have candy in the cabin. Mr. Jenkins had told them a week ago that sweets were absolutely *Against the Rules*! They might attract "critters," like mice or chipmunks, to the cabin.

Janna popped a cherry Life Saver in her mouth. She'd taken care of the critter problem by packing the candy in this tightly closed stuff sack. No smells could possibly get out, so the animals wouldn't even notice her candy. Hopefully, neither would anyone else. Janna adored secrets. "No tigers or bears in our cabin," she announced in a singsong voice.

"I hope not!" Anna replied, then said to Elizabeth, "Maybe you saw a squirrel."

Elizabeth turned to look suspiciously at Janna. "Bears don't live in Kansas anymore. And tigers never did."

Janna shrugged her shoulders. Then she grinned at her best friend — with lips closed, of course, so Elizabeth wouldn't see the candy.

The custodian bustled into the cabin. "Finish up quickly with your unpacking, girls. The other students are waiting to explore." Then she stared, openmouthed, at the pink rug by Janna's trunk.

"Yes, Mrs. Grand," the girls chorused, except for Janna. Janna blew her bangs off her forehead. She had never been able to understand why all the kids thought the custodian was so wonderful.

Janna hopped down off her bunk onto the fluffy rug and closed her trunk. Oops, the trunk wouldn't fit under the bottom bunk like the other girls' suitcases and backpacks. The only space was in the corner. That wasn't very convenient!

Janna dragged her trunk over to the corner as the other girls followed the custodian out of the cabin. Mrs. Grand began singing, "The foxes go marching two by

two, hurrah, hurrah!" The girls joined in the song.

Janna tugged harder. Having Mrs. Grand in charge of the girls' cabins might not be so bad. She would probably be spending a lot of her time with Micah. After all, he was her nephew.

Janna grinned as she slammed the cabin door and ran to catch up.

That meant she would have plenty of time, without an adult watching, to get into mischief.

And mischief was just as much fun as secrets!

3
A Bird on Her Head

Janna arrived first at the top of Ranger's Rock, panting like a racehorse. She'd beaten everyone else to the summit! Her swimming practice twice a week must be paying off. Janna hid behind a large boulder. When David trotted up the peak, she leaped out at him. "This is an ambush!" she yelled. "Give me all your bubble gum!" Janna pretended to throw him off the mountain until Mr. Jenkins and Mrs. Grand arrived, side by side.

"Leaping lizards and slithering snakes!"

the teacher exclaimed. He always used funny sayings when he was excited. "You can see all of Camp Buffalo from up here." Mr. Jenkins began motioning the children behind him to hurry. "Gather 'round, fearless campers. This is the time to tell you about the camp."

"The canoes on the lake look like little corks," Elizabeth said. Micah pointed out the cabins.

"I'll bet that's the Indian Mound," Mrs. Grand added, wiping her cheek with her bandana. Tom pretended to be an Indian, dancing around them all.

"You'll be visiting the Indian Mound first thing tomorrow morning," said Mr. Jenkins in his best teacher's voice so they could all hear. "The mound shows evidence that Indians used to live here on this land. For the next three days, Mrs. Grand and I and the camp counselors will be leading what I like to call Dazzling Discussions, filled with nature, news, and knowledge."

"Dreary discussions, you mean," David whispered.

Mr. Jenkins ignored him. "You'll be learning about wildlife, the prairie, and all the earlier peoples who lived in the *wilds* of Kansas. You'll have free time that you can spend in your cabins or at the lake." The teacher snapped his fingers. "You could even spend some free time practicing your skits. Don't forget, the skits need to have something to do with the animals or history of Kansas. We'll perform our plays Friday morning before we go back to school."

Janna had noticed a lone building in the middle of a meadow. She had to tug on Mr. Jenkins's sweater to get his attention. "What's that?"

"The Dove Cage," Mr. Jenkins answered. "It was just being built when I was here last year . . . to help students study the habits of birds up close and see their nests. Maybe we can ask one of the camp counselors to take you there."

17

As the rest of the class turned with Mr. Jenkins to try to spot the Pioneer Graveyard in the prairie, Janna grabbed Elizabeth's arm. "Let's go see the Dove Cage now!" she whispered.

Elizabeth twisted her hair around one finger doubtfully.

"Pretty please with a cherry on top?" Janna begged. She could nearly always convince Elizabeth to join an escapade. They ran down the mountain, hopping over the boulders.

Janna skidded to a stop in front of the bird cage. She had never seen a cage so big. The building had a real roof with shingles, but screened-in sides. Janna counted four doves, one flying and the others perched on the branches of a dead tree propped up inside. Why, the cage was almost the same size as Red Fox cabin. Four little birds had as much space as ten girls? That wasn't fair!

A screen door in the cage led into a little

entryway, and then a second door opened into the space where the birds lived. Janna had seen double doors before at the walk-in exhibits at the zoo. The animals were less likely to escape that way. Without giving herself a moment to think, Janna opened the door of the cage and scooted inside the entryway. She carefully latched the door behind her, so the birds would be safe.

"What are you doing?" Elizabeth asked. "Don't you think you should have permission to go in there?"

Janna opened the inner door and slipped inside — with the doves. The doves flew around above her head, flapping their wings. Janna held up her hand. "Don't be scared," she murmured gently, half to Elizabeth and half to the doves.

A dove landed on her outstretched finger. Janna could hardly breathe, she was so astonished. She knew she was grinning from ear to ear.

"Wow!" Elizabeth exclaimed.

The long claws gripped Janna's finger firmly, but didn't hurt her. Then the dove walked up her arm to her shoulder. It cocked its little head and looked in her ear! "Silly bird," Janna whispered. She could hear the sounds of other children entering the clearing.

"They're over here, Aunt Grace!" Micah called.

Traitor, Janna thought. The dove started crawling up her hair.

"Elizabeth! Janna!" Mr. Jenkins exclaimed. "You may not wander off without the rest of the class! Didn't I make that clear?"

"Yes, Mr. Jenkins," Elizabeth answered in her high-pitched embarrassed voice.

Janna twirled very carefully to look at her teacher. "Sorry," she said. "It was my fault." The bird's toenails pricked into her scalp.

Mr. Jenkins's glare softened. "Why, Janna," he said. "You have a bird sitting on top of your head." David chortled loudly, but Mr. Jenkins gestured at him to be quiet. Then he pulled out his camera. He crept closer and snapped a picture! "For our Camp Memory Board," he said.

4
Slithers Goes Visiting

Janna stood behind the bench at one of the long tables in the Dining Hall, right next to Elizabeth. She tugged Ribbit's head out the top of her sweatshirt so the stuffed frog could join her for dinner. All that fresh air had made Ribbit *starving*.

Rainbow, the camp counselor, led them singing a verse of "Kum Ba Yah." Elizabeth leaned over and patted Ribbit. Suddenly she nudged Janna and pointed at the buffalo head on the wall above Rainbow. The buffalo head was very old and used to belong to a real buffalo. It had been hanging in the Dining Hall forever. That's how Camp Buffalo had gotten its name.

Janna gasped. The buffalo was wearing her stuffed snake, Slithers, draped across its head! Slowly, students at the other tables started to point. At the end of the song, Rainbow leaned her head back. "Ah," she said. "Old Buffy seems to have made a new friend."

Janna stomped her foot and yelled above the growing merriment, "That's my snake!"

David grabbed his stomach and nearly fell over his bench as he began giggling. Mrs. Grand's cheeks turned red. She laughed so hard she had to wipe a tear away from one eye.

Janna rather liked all the attention. "Slithers!" she announced, putting her fists on her hips. "You're not supposed to wander all over camp by yourself." Janna tossed her ponytail over her shoulder and

glanced slyly at Mr. Jenkins. "Everybody has to stay with the group!"

Mr. Jenkins rolled his eyes and looked heavenward, but he laughed.

"Dinner's ready!" Rainbow called above the glee. "Hoppers, come up front, please."

Elizabeth and Tom, who had been chosen as hoppers from their table, trooped to the kitchen counter as everyone else took their seats. The hoppers brought back steaming platters of spaghetti and hot rolls. Then they returned for bowls of salad and applesauce.

No one could start eating until all the food had been served. Janna could barely resist nibbling on her hot roll. Ribbit almost stole a bite, too. Janna served herself a big plateful of spaghetti and passed the bowl on to Anna. If she didn't eat soon, she'd faint and slip off the bench! Finally the last person, Tom, scooped some salad onto his plate.

Janna ate her buttery roll first, closing her eyes in pleasure. As she rolled her pasta on her fork, she looked up again at her snake. Slithers's head hung down by the buffalo's nose, as if they were talking. Maybe they were sharing secrets.

How in all of America, or in all of Spain, had anyone managed to wrap Slithers neatly around the buffalo's ears? The buffalo head was ten feet off the ground! Even a girl or boy standing on a table wouldn't be able to reach so high. The only person tall enough to do that would be Mr. Jenkins. Janna considered that idea. Her teacher *did* like to tease, yet she couldn't imagine him sneaking into her cabin and taking Slithers off her bunk.

At least Slithers looked happy up high. Besides, she was on her way to becoming famous! Janna heard Elizabeth suggesting that a person might have pushed Slithers up there with a broom handle.

"Or maybe someone shot that snake up at the buffalo with an arrow . . . just like an Indian," Tom said, pretending to draw a bow.

Mr. Jenkins leaned over Janna during dessert and promised that he would find a ladder and get Slithers down tomorrow. Then the teacher walked to the front of the room, holding a telescope under his arm. "Red Foxes and Possums, you're with me!" Janna followed him sleepily out into the dark meadow, still munching her brownie.

"Look, Ribbit!" Janna exclaimed. "Have you ever *in your whole life* seen so many stars?" She showed her frog two constellations, the Big Dipper and the Seven Sisters. Mr. Jenkins explained that they could see more stars because they were far away from the city lights.

The most fantastic part of the evening turned out to be looking through the telescope. Janna could see the Man in the Moon as clearly as if he were right here at camp!

Finally Mr. Jenkins and Mrs. Grand leaned shoulder to shoulder and sang "Good Night, Campers" in perfect harmony. Janna yawned. Her teacher and the custodian seemed to be becoming awfully good friends. The girls headed one way and the boys the other way to their cabins.

Janna trooped into Red Fox. All the girls noisily put on their pajamas and crawled into their sleeping bags. That's when Janna realized how much she missed Slithers. She was used to the snake surrounding her every night. Now she had only her leopard and frog for company. Janna set Leppi on one side of her and Ribbit on the other.

Mrs. Grand opened each window a crack. The windows opened outward into the night. Then the custodian walked around the cabin, saying good night to every girl. When she came to Janna, she patted her shoulder. "That dove certainly liked you this afternoon."

Mrs. Grand flipped out the lights as she stepped into the counselor's nook and closed the door.

Janna rolled over to look out the window right beside her bunk. The other girls shone their flashlights wildly all over the walls and the ceiling. Janna's hands felt clammy . . . for no reason at all. She stared at the moon, clutching Leppi.

Janna couldn't believe it, but she missed Mama tucking her into bed. She even missed Mama singing her a Spanish song. Mama spoke Spanish at bedtime. She had been brought up in Spain, and she insisted that Janna and Manuel learn both English and Spanish.

Janna closed her eyes. Her family always drove her nuts! Yet there could only be one word for how she was feeling right now. She had all the symptoms. Her heart hurt. Her stomach had started flip-flopping like a pancake again. Her eyes even burned.

She should be thrilled to get away from her family for a few days.

Instead, here she was . . . feeling home-sick!

5
Night Surprise

Creeaaaakkkkk!

In her dream, Janna heard the sound. She was standing in the dressing room at the swimming pool on the first day of summer. The door to the pool was opening with a creak and letting in a blast of cold air. Janna shivered in her dream and pulled a beach towel from her pool bag. She wrapped the towel tightly around her shoulders.

Creeaakkk.

As the door swung wide, in strode an

animal — walking on two legs. Janna grinned. The animal looked like a teddy bear, a proud teddy bear.

What a funny dream I'm having, Janna thought.

The animal moved along, making rustling sounds. It had bright white stripes on the sides of its face. The creature lumbered right by her, so close that fur brushed her elbow.

"Hello, Mr. Bear," Janna said cheerily, in her dream.

"Greetings, Little Human," a scratchy voice replied. Then the creature reached into Janna's pool bag and pulled out her Life Savers. Janna couldn't believe it! The teddy bear crunched on a red Life Saver and batted a green one across the floor.

"Stop!" Janna cried, furious. "Those are mine!" She reached out to push the animal away. "Sto — "

Janna awakened in a strange bed. Then she remembered. She was in a top bunk at camp. But she was still shrieking *"Stop!"* at the top of her lungs. A million times worse . . . her hand was touching something *furry*.

Janna jerked her arm back and stopped shrieking in midword. A shadow leaned over her — a giant shadow! Janna ceased even breathing. A light flashed and for an instant she could see the creature clearly. The animal had black circles around its eyes like a mask. Janna could see claws on the upraised paw.

"A bear!" Janna wailed, rolling away to bury her face in her hands. Her heart pounded and thumped as if it would leap right out of her chest. Janna knew she was going to be eaten!

Then Janna felt the creature running down her side. One foot even stepped on her back. The window creaked again. Janna heard the sounds of an animal dropping to the ground outside and rushing away.

She opened one eye and gasped. Elizabeth was peering over her bunk, her eyes looking like flying saucers. Sidney crouched on the next top bunk with her flashlight on. The girl's mouth hung wide open. "There was a r-ra-raccoon on your bed!"

Janna's teeth chattered, and she was sure she had goose bumps the size of mountains. She sat up, glancing at the wall. Oh, no! Her little purple bag was *gone.*

"That raccoon stole my Life Savers!" she yelled, so loudly that her voice cracked. Janna grabbed her flashlight and shone the light out the window. There was no sign of the culprit. "Thief!" Janna yelled into the night.

Mrs. Grand rushed into the room from the counselor's nook and flipped on the overhead light. Her purple flannel nightgown billowed out behind her.

"Life Savers?" Elizabeth asked, blinking.

At that very moment, Janna remembered that she wasn't supposed to have candy at camp. She couldn't seem to swallow.

Janna had to explain her nightmare, not once, but over and over. She couldn't believe how upset everyone got. And no one, no one at all, cared about her Life Savers!

Mrs. Grand seemed most worried about the candy attracting an animal. Some of the girls were upset because the raccoon might have bitten them. Anna even started sobbing.

Mr. Jenkins stomped up the stairs to the cabin. He looked funny standing outside the screen door in his red striped pajamas and boots. His hair stuck up on the top of his head. The teacher was quite disturbed by the fuss. Everyone in the whole camp seemed to be wide awake. Not only all the girls, but the boys as well. Janna could hear laughter from one of the boys' cabins.

After Janna repeated her story again, Mr. Jenkins announced from the doorway, "Janna, you broke the rules this afternoon by running off from the group. Now I discover that you sneaked candy into the cabin. So this is the *second* example of your clearly breaking the rules. If you break the rules one more time, I'll . . . I'll call your parents."

Janna's lip quivered. Her chin wobbled. This was too much. She gazed at her teacher and burst into tears. "I don't have Slithers," she wailed. "I've lost my Life Savers! And you want to call my p-p-parents?"

Elizabeth squeezed Janna's fingers, and Sidney wiped a tear away from her own eye.

Mr. Jenkins opened his mouth as if he wanted to speak, but no words came out. He lifted his hands in the air, astonished.

"Now look what you've done," Mrs. Grand exclaimed, and gently shooed the teacher down the front stairs of the cabin.

Then Mrs. Grand picked up a book. She began to read aloud. The story was about a girl named Lucy who walked through a wardrobe and visited a magical land. Anna quit sobbing. Janna stopped sniffling to listen, too. The custodian turned out the overhead light and shone a flashlight on the book. She read long into the night.

Janna finally fell asleep to the rhythm of the custodian's soft voice.

6

The Nutty Clue

The blaring notes of Anna playing reveille on her trumpet shook Janna awake the next morning. She felt the sound from the tips of her toes to her eyeballs. Even her teeth rattled. She did *not* want to get out of her warm sleeping bag.

Janna muttered weakly, "Camp Buffalo, here I come." She rolled onto her stomach and slid feet first off the bunk. Janna yanked her fluffy green towel out of her trunk, then grabbed her otter-shaped soap and clean clothes. She slipped into her mermaid slippers and shuffled to the showers.

Fifteen minutes later, Janna strolled back into the cabin, ready for the second camp day. *"Buenas dias,"* she called to Sidney, who was up on a top bunk straightening out her sleeping bag. "Great trumpet playing," she added to Anna.

Anna stared at her feet.

Janna looked around the cabin in surprise. Why, everyone seemed to be ignoring her! Could the girls be mad at her . . . just because of one little raccoon with a great sense of smell?

A shiver scooted up Janna's back. She didn't like this new development, not one eensy bit. Janna hung her damp towel on the corner of her bunk and stuffed her dirty clothes in a plastic bag. Then she put everything else away. At least Mrs. Grand couldn't get upset at her for being messy.

Only Elizabeth waited for her to go to breakfast. Janna switched off the cabin lights, then the two friends stepped out onto the porch. Elizabeth leaned over and picked something up. "Look, a peanut!"

Janna wondered how a peanut could be exciting, a *ridiculous* nut. She scuffed her feet, like she always did when she was feeling sorry for herself. That's when she noticed peanuts scattered all over the steps . . . lots of them. The sight reminded Janna of how she had helped build a trap to catch Squeaks in the gym on Carnival Night last fall. They had made a ramp out of blocks and then put a row of sunflower seeds up the ramp to tempt Squeaks.

Had someone dropped all these peanuts on purpose, too?

Elizabeth zipped around the cabin one way. Janna darted in the other direction, searching for more peanuts in the pine needles and bushes. She only found a few nuts right by the porch. They met under the window by their bunk beds.

"Lizzy," Janna said slowly, using her friend's nickname. "Do you think someone *wanted* an animal to visit our cabin?"

Elizabeth lifted her right shoulder and crossed her arms in her detective look. Elizabeth loved to solve mysteries, particularly ones that involved animals. She had even started her own company called Pipsqueak Detective Agency. "The raccoon probably followed the peanuts onto our porch, *then* smelled your Life Savers."

"And being so smart, the raccoon preferred Life Savers!" Janna exclaimed. "Let's go tell the other girls that last night wasn't all my fault!"

Elizabeth caught her arm. "If there is a trickster," she whispered mysteriously, "perhaps we should try to catch the sneak ourselves."

The word *trickster* reminded Janna of the Dining Hall. Maybe the same person who had dropped these peanuts had hung her snake up on the buffalo yesterday! Janna's belly felt as if it were sliding down a water slide. Could both of the tricks have been aimed at her?

The Dining Hall bell rang through the

forest. *Clang, bong!* That meant they only had five minutes to get to breakfast! *Bong, clang.* Janna slipped her arm through Elizabeth's and they started to skip. Janna had to admit that Elizabeth's idea of catching the trickster was awfully tempting. The two of them could be looking for clues while they were at camp.

Best of all, Janna knew she would have a new secret. She just hoped the other girls would get over being so mad at her. "Let's do it, Lizzy!" Janna exclaimed. "Let's solve this mystery ourselves and not tell another soul."

Elizabeth grinned and half bowed. "Detective Elizabeth at your service."

Janna swung her free arm as high as the gray clouds in the sky as she skipped down the path. Still, she couldn't help wondering . . . what would the Camp Buffalo trickster do next?

7

A Froggy Friend

The wind whipped through Janna's hair as she stood by the edge of the pond. She hadn't heard more than five words of Mr. Jenkins's Dazzling Discussion about the Miami tribe of the Osage Indians that used to live in Kansas. Rainbow's Treehouse Talk about trees that grew on the edge of the prairie hadn't interested Janna very much either.

But this . . .

As Mrs. Grand spoke to them about the ecosystem of a pond, Janna carefully scooted sideways to the edge of the group. In a few moments, she stood by herself, the toes of her tennis shoes sinking satisfyingly into the mud. She liked looking at the tall dried grasses and the rocks. Some spring plants floated in the middle of the pond.

Too bad Elizabeth hadn't been in her group this morning. They couldn't even make plans about the trickster. Janna glanced back at the others. Micah had picked up a long stick and was pointing out the cattails as his aunt talked. He had on a neat, clean yellow shirt that looked as if it had just been ironed.

Janna took a deep breath. The pond smelled swampy, like the water in the flower vase at home if Mama left the flowers too long. She always kept cut flowers in the house. "Beauty makes for a loving home," Mama liked to say.

Janna sighed. She hoped Mama was getting along all right without her.

Something flew by Janna's knees and

landed with a little splash on the other side of a nearby rock.

What was that?

Janna wanted to explore, yet she hesitated. Surely Mr. Jenkins wouldn't count being twenty feet away from the group as breaking the rules. She *should* stay and listen. Janna's curiosity won the battle. If Mrs. Grand asked, she'd say she was investigating a sound.

Janna jumped onto the rock. Then she crouched down, pulling the dry reeds aside so she could see better. In the watery brown mud rested a dark green frog.

"You must be a full-grown frog," Janna whispered in a friendly voice. "It's too early in the spring for anything other than eggs."

Janna couldn't imagine spending a winter buried down in the squishy, icky mud of this pond. Still, she figured a pond this size must seem like a mansion to a frog.

With another little splash, the frog hopped nearer to her feet. Thrilled, Janna leaned closer. She could even see the eyes bulging out of the top of its head. Janna didn't try to touch the frog. Wild animals didn't like being petted. "Was the winter tough, girl?"

The frog sprang up again. Janna grinned. Maybe hopping meant yes. The frog hopped about as high as Janna's knees before plopping back into the mud. "I'll call you Tuffy," Janna said. "Do you like that name?"

Clearly, Tuffy was delighted. The frog hopped so high she almost touched Janna's nose. This time, the frog landed about an inch from her right tennis shoe.

"What are you doing?" Tom interrupted from the shore.

Janna glanced over her shoulder and put her finger over her lips. She didn't want the rest of the kids to notice.

"Tell me what you found," Tom begged softly.

Janna shrugged, considering. Her first instinct was to keep Tuffy a secret, but she didn't think it would do any harm to tell Tom. He was a nice boy. He liked her jokes. "Promise you won't tell?"

Tom nodded and made a cross over his heart.

"I'm making friends with a frog," Janna explained.

Tom leaped onto her rock. He landed so gracefully that the frog didn't even get spooked. Studying ballet had taught him to move as silently as an Indian. Tom crouched beside Janna.

"Tuffy, meet Tom," Janna whispered.

"Hi, Tuffy," Tom said politely. He reached out to pat the frog.

Instantly Tuffy bounded into her best jump yet . . . *away* from them. "You scared her!" Janna cried, glaring at Tom.

Tuffy splashed wildly into the middle of the pond, then scooted onto a log. Janna remembered reading that frogs could lay ten thousand eggs. She waved at the little creature. "May you have ten thousand babies this year, Tuffy." As if in reply, the little frog hopped one last time.

Tom clutched his forehead. "Yow! Can you imagine having nine thousand, nine hundred and ninety-nine brothers and sisters?" His mom had remarried this year and he now had two new brothers, along with his sisters. Everybody knew he was tired of brothers and sisters.

Janna ignored Tom's moaning. She stood up and called, *"Adios,* Tuffy!" The frog vanished into the cattails across the pond. Janna crossed her arms and hugged her ribs. Truth be told, she felt happy. She'd made a new friend this morning, a froggy friend.

8
Canoeing

Janna and Elizabeth arrived at the far shore of the lake just in time to claim the second canoe. All of the third-graders had one hour of free time after lunch. David and Tom were already paddling the first canoe out into the middle. Rainbow instructed the girls in basic canoe safety, then they slipped their life preservers on over their sweatshirts. Elizabeth pulled up her hood. The day had turned overcast and windy, and Janna knew she hated being cold.

Micah skidded into the clearing just as Janna chose a paddle that fit under her shoulder. She was trying very hard to act as if she knew what she was doing, even though she'd never in her life been in a canoe. Micah's face looked bright red from running. He glanced around, disappointed. "Are the canoes gone already?"

"Why don't you come with us," Elizabeth suggested. "There's room for three." She looked questioningly at Janna.

Actually, Janna didn't want to share. She'd been planning on having private detective time with Elizabeth to talk about the camp trickster. She had some theories about where the trickster might strike next . . . maybe at the Dove Cage or the Pioneer Graveyard. They couldn't have a secret discussion with Micah along, for goodness' sake! Still, Micah looked so hopeful. Janna sighed. "Sure."

Micah tucked in his yellow shirt. "Good, I want to look for evidence of duck nests."

Elizabeth crawled into the front seat,

and Micah took the middle. That meant Janna got the stern. She slipped her paddle into the boat as Rainbow had suggested. Then she took three running steps in the shallow water and pushed off as hard as she could. The canoe wobbled alarmingly as she jumped in.

"Good luck!" Rainbow called. "Remember, the person in the stern steers."

So Janna paddled as hard as she could. Water splashed up all around her. The canoe spun in circles. She was supposed to be in charge of steering this thing? Janna's arms ached, so she hesitated. Paddling like a mad girl hadn't worked. Janna looked at her friend to see what she was doing. Then Janna stuck her paddle in the water on the opposite side of the canoe from Elizabeth's paddle and pulled more slowly. Now, the boat weaved along in an S curve. "Yippee!" Janna cried. This was better than circles.

Slowly, Janna made the canoe swerve toward the other boat. She hadn't seen

David very much today. It would be fun to talk to him. Besides, she and Tom had a secret. As she neared the other boat, David called out in a singsong voice, "Janna made friends with a frog. Janna made friends with a frooogggg."

Micah looked up. "What frog?"

Janna stared at Tom, so astonished that she forgot to paddle. Tom had promised this morning not to tell anyone!

Tom half hid behind his paddle, his face flushing until his ears looked like strawberries. Yet the next instant, he grinned at Micah and answered him in a loud voice, "Ruffy is the frog's name."

Janna put her paddle in the water and pulled hard, aiming right for their boat. "Tuffy!" she corrected. The canoe shot forward. As Janna glided alongside the other canoe, she tried to poke Tom with her paddle. She missed, and they sailed on past.

"Did you say Muffy?" Micah asked, perfectly serious. He was the only one not laughing.

"No!" Tom howled. "I said Fluffy!"

David cried out, "I think I'll write a story about Janna and Puffy."

Janna's grip tightened on her paddle as she bit down on her lower lip. David was *good* at writing stories. Too good! Not only that, he loved to exaggerate! She didn't want a story written about her liking a frog. Her classmates might tease her forever. Janna spun their canoe back around and accidentally on purpose splashed the boys with her paddle. They ducked.

"Canoes!" Rainbow called from the bank, her hands cupped around her mouth so the sound would be amplified. "Separate, please! You are too close to each other."

Elizabeth and Micah turned their heads obediently to look at the counselor, but Janna felt as if she had a little volcano in her chest. Without thinking, she twisted her paddle through the water in a J shape so the canoe would draw closer to the boys. "You wouldn't dare write that story!"

she yelled at David. As Janna drifted near, she reached for the other canoe and missed.

"Stop, you two," Elizabeth begged in a whisper.

"Oh, wouldn't I?" David teased Janna. He was the only one still laughing. "Who else would make friends with a frog? You might even kiss a frog!"

Janna could feel the volcano inside her steaming up, then exploding in a fiery heat. David was making fun of her! He was making fun of Tuffy, too, a poor little frog. She'd show him! Janna stood up and lunged for the other canoe.

"Sit down!" Micah and Elizabeth yelled together. The canoe wobbled to the right. Tom covered his eyes with his arm.

Janna gasped. She grabbed for the sides of the boat with both hands and accidentally dropped her paddle. It floated away, out of reach. Now how was she going to steer? The canoe rocked to the left, then rolled to the right in a wild bouncing dance.

"Help!" Micah yelped.

"Oh, boy," Elizabeth muttered. "Oh, girl."

Janna screamed as the canoe flipped over and dumped all three of them into the lake. The water felt cold as ice. Janna bobbed right up to the surface in her life preserver. She sputtered and opened her eyes to pitch-blackness.

What had happened? Where was she?

Janna waved her arms, panic-stricken. Her left hand thumped into something hard. Janna stopped thrashing. She must be inside the turned-over canoe! Janna ducked under the edge and swam into the open air. She could see the lake again and the boys' canoe. What a relief! She could even see Rainbow jumping into the rescue rowboat at the shore.

David's and Tom's voices called out as one, "Are you all right?" They both sounded worried, really worried.

Elizabeth bobbed up next and glared at Janna in pure fury. Her teeth chattered,

and her light brown skin looked gray.

Micah came to the surface last, clutching his glasses fearfully. Algae dripped off the collar of his yellow shirt. Rainbow rowed the rescue boat right up to him.

Janna didn't feel all hot and fiery anymore. The icy water had washed away the volcano inside her. She had a horrible sinking feeling that this accident might be considered all her fault. Elizabeth grabbed one side of the canoe. Janna grabbed the other side and started meekly swimming to shore.

9
Peanut Butter and Jelly Friends

Janna leaned closer to the warmth of the fire in the large stone fireplace in the Dining Hall. The flames looked bluish purple with a bit of yellow on the edges. She'd never realized before that fire wasn't truly red.

Elizabeth had been completely silent since their canoe had flipped. Janna had said she was sorry right after she had stumbled onto shore. While they showered, Janna had even tried telling a joke about how they'd been in the water so much they might turn into mermaids if they weren't careful. Elizabeth had just kept on sighing. Now she wasn't even drinking her hot chocolate. That was a *bad* sign.

Janna nibbled on her fingernail. On top of it all, she wasn't certain what Mr. Jenkins would do when he arrived. He'd call her parents for sure. Janna started chewing on her thumbnail. Maybe he'd even send her home. That would be lots scarier than dumping the canoe. She wouldn't mind going home, but she didn't want to be sent home. Janna imagined that Dad would yell and say she couldn't go to the movies with her friends next week.

Worse than that, Mama would quietly tell her how disappointed she was, in Spanish. All serious talks happened in Spanish. Mama would fix some tea and they would talk for hours about how Janna was responsible for her own actions. Responsi-*pill*-ity, Janna liked to say, under her breath.

The door to the Dining Hall slammed. Micah rushed toward the fire, all hunched over. His neatly combed wet hair dripped water down his neck. Micah sat down beside Elizabeth, sharing the corner of her chair. He reached for his cup of hot chocolate and cradled it in his hands.

Janna dared a glance at him. Hey, he looked cheerful! Micah was staring at the buffalo head on the wall above them. "Perhaps Slithers should be our camp mascot," he said. "She could just stay up there on the buffalo's head until we leave."

Janna picked up a graham cracker. "Slithers *is* a clever snake." Then Janna got brave and added, "Right, Elizabeth?"

Elizabeth silently drew a picture of a boat in the dust on the side of the fireplace.

"American Indians think of the snake as a wise creature," Micah said. "Maybe Slithers could give us advice."

I could sure use some of that, Janna thought.

"She might give advice by telling stories," Micah continued. "Slithers, the Storytelling Snake. I wonder what story she would tell us about canoes." He grinned. "That was quite an adventure we had on the lake. We barely survived with our lives."

"Flipping over canoes *is* a serious business," Mr. Jenkins agreed, right behind them.

Janna nearly tossed her hot chocolate in the air, she was so surprised. She turned toward her teacher. She wanted to say that this whole awful mess wasn't *really* her fault, no matter how it looked. She'd been planning on giving Mr. Jenkins her best grin, tossing her ponytail over her shoulder and blaming David. But Janna found she couldn't even swallow, let alone talk. She had too many *worry bugs* crawling around inside her, as Manuel liked to say.

The teacher sat down on the hearth and snagged three graham crackers. Janna begged him with her eyes. He didn't say anything. He just gazed back at her, as quiet as a mouse. That's when Janna understood. Making this situation better was all up to her. For once, she'd better not try to make everyone laugh. "I didn't think about what would happen when I stood up in the boat," she admitted. "A volcano just exploded — bang! — inside me."

Mr. Jenkins nibbled thoughtfully.

But Elizabeth was looking at Janna, truly looking at her. So Janna tried even harder. "I really am sorry. I'm afraid it was . . . was . . ." Janna was having trouble saying the words. She'd had no idea being honest was so hard. "Oh!" she exclaimed. "It was all my fault."

"David was teasing you," Micah replied.

"We were all teasing you," Elizabeth added.

"That boy made me mad, mad, *mad,*" Janna agreed, clenching her hands into fists. She felt her face getting warm. Then she thought of Mama. "But even David didn't force me to leap to my feet. No one else controls *my* feet." She turned to Mr. Jenkins. "How about if next time I try to think first?"

"Well!" Mr. Jenkins waved his graham cracker in the air. "This is a special day. You're growing up, Janna." He patted her shoulder. "And in honor of that, I'm not going to call your parents."

Janna gasped.

"But your canoe privileges are hereby revoked. No more boating!" Mr. Jenkins stood up. "Finish your snack, you three, and get toasty warm. Then join us at the Indian Mound." He started to walk away, then pulled something out of his jacket pocket. "Pokey possums, I almost forgot! You missed mail call while you were showering." He handed each of them a letter.

"Oh, thank you, Mr. Jenkins," Janna said, clutching her letter to her chest. For a moment she felt like crying. Her letter smelled just like Mama's favorite perfume.

Micah opened his envelope. He unfolded a picture, a watercolor scene of what looked like flying hamburgers. There wasn't even a note, but Micah laughed uproariously. His father, the artist, must have painted the scene.

Janna recognized Mama's handwriting as she ripped open her own envelope. Mama wrote about how the family was going to make chicken enchiladas for dinner. Janna smiled when she came to the last line. Mama had written in Spanish, *I love you, "Te amo."* At the bottom, Dad had added six O's for hugs and five X's for kisses. Her little twerp of a brother had even drawn a funny picture of himself with hands as big as shovels.

Sighing, Janna slipped the letter into her back pocket to keep it safe. Then she glanced at Elizabeth out of the side of her eyes. Oops. Everything wasn't all better yet. "Lizzy?" Janna whispered. What in the world was she going to say? Then she remembered what they used to chant together when they were little kids. Only this time, Janna turned it into a question,

"Good friends,
Best friends,
Peanut butter
and jelly friends?"

"Stop calling me Lizzy!" Elizabeth exclaimed, but Janna thought she saw one side of Elizabeth's mouth curling up into a grin.

10
Bedtime Stories

At the Indian Mound, Mr. Jenkins sneaked up on Elizabeth with his camera while she was pretending to be an archaeologist. He was taking more pictures for the Camp Memory Board the third-graders were going to set up in the hallway between their classrooms. Janna had already started creating a quote in her mind for her picture in the Dove Cage.

At dinner, David and Micah carried a giant platter of cinnamon rolls to their table together. David wore a red cap backward on his head. To everyone's glee, Micah snatched Tom's hat and put it on backward, too. Then Mr. Jenkins snapped their picture.

The teacher seemed to be everywhere with his camera. He caught Sidney and Rainbow striking the match and lighting the night campfire. He crept up behind Mrs. Grand as she swayed back and forth and waved her arms, leading the singing.

After the campfire, Janna and the other girls tickled and poked each other as they headed back to Red Fox. None of the girls had any intention of going to sleep, so three of them took long steamy showers while Janna and the rest made plans.

Janna put on her pajamas as slowly as she could. She arranged Ribbit and Leppi, but she didn't climb onto her bunk. She was folding her towel perfectly into her trunk when Mrs. Grand came in for the third time. "I'm turning out the lights now!" the custodian exclaimed, looking frazzled. "It's after ten o'clock!"

The cabin sank into darkness. Janna pulled her flashlight out of the waistband of her pajamas. Then she counted to sixty. This part of the plan had been her idea. The other girls must be counting, too, for the cabin stayed miraculously silent.

"That's much better, girls. Good night!" the custodian said, stepping into the counselor's nook and closing the door behind her.

Almost immediately, Janna heard the shower running. She snapped on her flashlight mischievously. This was the perfect plot. There was no way she could get in trouble for something every girl was doing. "We did it!"

"Come on over, Foxes," Sidney said, giggling. "It's time for stories."

They all gathered on Elizabeth's bed. Janna scrunched against the wall, holding Elizabeth's little seal. Her whole body tingled with excitement. With a giggle, Janna started a story about Elizabeth's seal going out for ice cream. Each girl added a sentence. By the end of the story, the seal swam in a bathtub of swirling Malted Milk Ball ice cream. Janna put one hand firmly over her mouth so she wouldn't howl.

Then Anna told a story about her brother meeting a bear in the woods. "He really did!" Anna insisted loudly, while everyone whispered, "Shhhhh!" Anna bounced on the bed. "Gerald screamed and the bear roared, and they ran in different directions."

That story wasn't quite so funny, but Elizabeth put a flashlight in her mouth and lit up her face. All the girls began imitating her.

"Now it's time for ghost stories!" Sidney exclaimed.

"I don't like ghost stories," Anna answered.

"Me, neither," Lea seconded.

Sidney ignored them. "Once upon a time, a girl went into an old abandoned house. She crept up the stairs." Sidney leaned forward into the middle of the circle of nightgowned girls and imitated the sounds: *"CREAK. CREEEAK. CREEEAAAKKK!*

"That's it," Anna announced. "I'm going to bed."

One by one, each girl crept into her own bed as the story got scarier. Elizabeth covered her head with her pillow. Finally Janna discovered she was the only one left listening. Janna liked being scared, but she stayed mostly because Sidney had hold of her hands in a tight grip.

"The girl ran all the way home on that dark, moonless night . . . with the ghost *following* her," Sidney whispered in her creepiest voice.

Janna's fingers and toes felt icy. Actually, the story wasn't so frightening. It was the *way* Sidney told the story. Despite herself, Janna shivered. She wished the wind would stop rattling the branches of the trees outside the dark cabin.

"Thennnn . . ." Sidney stretched out the word, "the ghost became the girl's secret friend!" she exclaimed cheerfully. "And lived with her forever. Each Halloween, the ghost went trick-or-treating with her!" Sidney laughed at the punch line. "It was a friendly ghost all along!"

Janna laughed, too, but the sound came out more like a strangled gulp.

"That's not funny," Elizabeth muttered from underneath her pillow. "You scared us all."

Sidney scrambled up into her own bed, giggling merrily.

Janna sat close to Elizabeth until her heart stopped pounding so hard. The cabin became more and more silent as the other girls slowly fell asleep. Janna put her flashlight in her teeth so she could use both hands and began climbing up the ladder onto her own bed. She'd have to remember Sidney's story, word for word, so she could tell Manuel.

Janna sat on her pillow and slipped her right leg into her sleeping bag. She would practice the story on her little brother until she got really good at terrifying him. Then she'd tell the story to other people. Being a ghostly storyteller was a great idea. Mama always said she should have goals. Janna slipped her left leg into her sleeping bag and started to wiggle down.

Something touched her foot.

A ghost? Janna thought. She froze, then half grinned at herself. *Surely not.* She must still be scared from Sidney's story. Janna snuggled deeper into her warm bag.

That's when something wiggled beside her leg. Something very clammy.

Janna squealed . . . yet the sound came out a breathy squeak.

Janna figured she might die. Her heart would stop beating, and she would die from fright.

Slowly Janna lifted up the opening of her sleeping bag and shone the light inside.

It took Janna a moment to see the body

. . . and the tiny legs by her leg . . . and finally, the bulging eyes.

Janna blinked. She couldn't believe what she saw. "There's a frog in my sleeping bag!" she yelled.

11
Back to the Mansion

The last sight Janna had seen as she screeched was the frog hopping deeper inside her sleeping bag. *Hopping!* Janna lay now in absolute blackness. She'd dropped her flashlight. She swallowed, fumbling for the light with one hand, careful not to move her legs even a millimeter. None of the other girls seemed to be awake. She must not have yelled as loudly as she had thought.

Elizabeth's head popped up over her bunk just as Janna found her flashlight and snapped it on again. She accidentally shone the glaring light in her friend's eyes. Elizabeth blinked. Janna swept the beam of light inside her sleeping bag. By her knee rested a dark green shape, a small shape.

Why, the frog looked just like Tuffy!

Janna dropped her flashlight on her stomach and scooped up the frog in her hands. "Poor squirt," she whispered. "You must be terrified."

"And you're not?" Sidney hissed, as she crawled from her top bunk to Janna's.

"Me, scared of a tiny frog?" The frog in Janna's hands tried to hop, and it tickled. "I must be a hundred times bigger than this little tyke." Janna glanced around the dark room. None of the other girls had even rolled over.

Janna moved her cupped hands into the beam of Elizabeth's flashlight and peered between her fingers. Could this really be Tuffy?

The frog was about the same size, and

there was something about the eyes that looked the same. Janna nibbled on her lower lip. She felt that heart-clutching feeling she often got when she saw a lonely animal. She wanted . . . no, she *needed* . . . to bring this adorable animal home. Janna sighed. Mama would not appreciate her coming home from camp with a frog. Janna could try to hide it, maybe set up a secret pond in her closet. But that wouldn't last for long. Mama was too smart. Besides, Trashtruck, her ex-alley cat, might try to eat Tuffy.

No . . . Janna had to admit that taking the frog home wouldn't work.

At that moment, the door to the counselor's nook started to creak open. Elizabeth dove into her bed. Janna flipped off her light. She crumpled over sideways, carefully cradling the frog in her hands. Janna kept one eye slitted open just enough to see.

Mrs. Grand stood in the doorway, peering around the room. Then she stepped back into her nook, her dark figure disappearing as she closed the door.

"Whew!" Sidney breathed, and turned on her light.

Elizabeth stood back up. "Who knew you had made friends with a frog?" she whispered.

"Friends with a frog?" Sidney asked.

"Micah knew . . . and Tom," Elizabeth continued, answering her own question. She crossed her arms in her detective look. "Not to mention David!"

"Shhh," Janna warned, her heart pounding. For goodness' sake, Mrs. Grand might come back! Janna definitely didn't want any adults involved in this, like last night. She was beginning to come up with a plan. Besides, she didn't want the rest of the Red Foxes to wake up. Anna and Lea might make a racket.

Janna handed the frog to Elizabeth. "Hold Tuffy while I get down."

Elizabeth's eyes nearly popped out of her head as she cradled the little green creature in her hands, but she didn't drop it.

Janna slid silently off her bunk. She pulled on her tennis shoes and her jacket.

"What are you doing?" Elizabeth's face had puckered with distaste. The frog must be wiggling.

"I . . . I mean, *we* . . . are taking Tuffy back to the pond, of course." Janna carefully took the frog from Elizabeth. "Better grab your coat. It's windy outside."

"Nothing doing," Elizabeth replied.

"I can't carry Tuffy and hold a flashlight," Janna insisted. She begged, "I need your help, and you're my *best* friend."

"You sneak." Elizabeth rolled her eyes. But she slipped on her shoes. "One of these days you are going to get me into awful trouble."

Sidney agreed to stuff their sleeping bags with clothes so it looked as if they were still in bed in case anyone woke up.

Janna and Elizabeth crept out of the cabin and into the dark night, trying not

to step on the squeakiest part of the stairs. Janna tiptoed down the path. The frog felt slimy between her hands.

"How did you talk me into this?" Elizabeth muttered behind her.

The cold crept up inside the sleeves of Janna's jacket. An owl hooted, and she almost jumped out of her skin. She and Elizabeth sneaked past all the cabins, then past the Dining Hall. Janna could hear the frogs croaking in the moonlight from the nearby pond. Then all the frogs fell silent, and Janna knew it was because they could hear her coming.

Janna knelt by the side of the pond in the mud and opened her hands. "Bye, Tuffy," she whispered. Her knees squelched in the mud. "Are you going to enjoy your froggy mansion?"

Tuffy hopped in agreement. She landed right beside Janna's hands.

"I'm too big to come with you," Janna whispered. Then she said in Spanish, *I'll miss you, "Te extrañaré."*

Elizabeth poked her shoulder. "Come on. We have to go!" her voice rose.

Janna watched Tuffy bound into the air. She heard a little splash, but couldn't see where the frog had landed. Then, from all sides of the pond, Janna heard the croaking again, even louder this time. All the other frogs must be welcoming Tuffy home!

"I don't know about you," Elizabeth insisted, "but I don't want to get grounded for the rest of my life."

They hurried back to the Dining Hall, then Elizabeth snapped off her flashlight. To Janna's amazement, she found she could see just fine. Her eyes must have adapted to the dim moonlight.

Janna crept past the Squirrel cabin. Going back seemed much more frightening, perhaps because she wasn't concentrating on Tuffy. Her footsteps sounded as loud as an elephant loose in a forest. She stepped on a twig, and it *cracked*! Janna froze. What if Mr. Jenkins was a light sleeper?

Janna didn't even want to imagine what would happen to Elizabeth and to her if they got caught. She didn't think her teacher ever boiled his students in oil, but she wasn't completely sure. Janna raced up the stairs to Red Fox, her heart pounding in her dry throat.

Sidney already had the door open for them. "All clear," she whispered. "Did the mission go smoothly?"

Janna nodded. She slipped off her shoes and jacket, her hands trembling. She knew she had done the right thing to take Tuffy back to the pond. Still, right now she was afraid her knees wouldn't hold her up for another second. Janna tried to wipe the mud off her pajamas. Then she gave up. She'd just have to hope Mrs. Grand didn't notice.

Janna hugged Elizabeth, then scrambled up into her own bed. She crawled inside and pulled her sleeping bag over her head.

Janna's last thought before she fell into an exhausted sleep was that tomorrow, when she was wide awake again, she'd have to figure out just who had played this trick on her!

Then Janna dreamed all night long of being a frog. She dreamed that she loved to play hopping games in her pond mansion. Statues of flies filled her rooms, and lily pad wallpaper covered her muddy walls.

12
Buffy Tells All

The final morning of camp began with the blaring notes of Anna playing reveille on her trumpet once again. Janna dressed quickly. Then she sauntered to the Dining Hall, pretending to be as relaxed as a lizard sunning on a rock. She figured that whoever had put the frog in her sleeping bag had expected her to scream and wake up the entire camp last night. Janna felt extremely proud of her crafty silence. The trickster must be absolutely *dying* of curiosity by now.

Janna waved good morning to Slithers, then slid onto a bench. The hoppers carried heaping bowls of plump raisins and brown sugar to the table. They brought tall pitchers of cool milk. The oatmeal tasted delicious . . . even though Janna usually thought of hot cereal in the same category as brussels sprouts.

After breakfast, Janna hiked alone to the Dove Cage. The students had one final hour of free time at Camp Buffalo. The air smelled fresh and sharp, like new flowers. Once inside the Dove Cage, Janna lifted both arms like a scarecrow. To her delight, a bird landed on each of her outstretched hands. She decided to call the dusty-colored one on her right Silky. The birds started walking up her arms, their tiny feet prickling into her skin. The dove now on her left elbow made bubbly, tuneful coos. She'd call that one Coo. Coo flapped into the air and landed on her head. Janna stood like a statue and let her eyes slip out of focus.

From the corner of her right eye, she could see Silky on her arm. The bird looked so pretty that he seemed to have a light shining inside him . . . like the rainbow on her kitchen wall made from sunlight shining through Mama's crystal hanging in the window. Janna grinned. Did she have a rainbow light shining inside of her, too? She liked to think of herself as shining with rainbow colors . . . red, orange, yellow, green, blue, purple, and violet. Silky spread her dusty wings and cocked her head to look at Janna with one beady little eye.

Much too soon, the *Come Back Now!* bell from the Dining Hall clanged a warning through the forest. Silky and Coo leaped into the air at the loud sound, flapping up to perch in a high corner. Janna let herself out of the cage, then raced to the Dining Hall. She and Elizabeth and Micah had planned a skit together, and they had to practice one last time. Janna and Elizabeth hoped that their skit would draw the trickster from the crowd.

David and Sidney and Anna acted out their skit first, pretending to be animals who lived in the woods. David was a squirrel. He'd made little ears that attached to a headband, and he wore a long gray bushy tail made from the sleeve of a sweater. Sidney had painted black eyes and white stripes on her face to make herself look like a raccoon, and Anna became a deer. Their play was about people building houses deeper into their woods and ruining their habitats.

Then Mr. Jenkins and Mrs. Grand and Tom pretended to be pioneers who came to Kansas in covered wagons. Mr. Jenkins and Tom built a sod house. Mrs. Grand began pretending to nail together a wooden cabin for herself.

"Why don't you just get married?" Janna called. "Then you wouldn't *need* another cabin."

The whole class giggled. Janna tossed her ponytail over her shoulder. These skits were turning out to be the best part of camp.

"Can't you be quiet for once?" Micah exclaimed, and shoved her.

Janna stared at Micah, startled. Micah had never once pushed her, or anyone else that she could remember. Why was he so upset that his face looked like a purple tomato? It was just *funny* to think of Mr. Jenkins and Mrs. Grand being married. This wasn't anything to get mad about.

Then Janna hesitated thoughtfully. She wasn't sure, but Mrs. Grand might be divorced. The custodian's cheeks turned red.

Mr. Jenkins stood looking at his boots. He had told them once at the beginning of the year that his wife had died years ago. His daughter, Amy, had grown up and started college this year. So he *must* be lonely. Janna clapped along with the rest when the skit was finished. She'd have to give this idea further thought.

Janna and Elizabeth and Micah took

their places in front of the fireplace, because Slithers the Storytelling Snake and Buffy the Buffalo were characters in their skit. Micah spoke for Slithers and Elizabeth for Buffy.

Janna pretended to be an ancient counselor who'd been at the camp for a hundred years. She leaned on a cane made out of a stick and spoke in a wavering voice. "Long, long ago, campers, I remember when the biggest black bear you ever saw wandered in to visit this dining hall."

The three friends acted out the whole story of the bear visiting camp. At the end, they finished the skit with a scene of a camper who put a snake into a cabin to scare kids. Janna and Elizabeth had planned this part carefully, hoping it would make the trickster react and give himself away.

When they bowed, the third-graders laughed and cheered. Janna and Elizabeth watched the audience. Anna just clapped her hands politely. David waved his squirrel tail. Tom danced around, pretending to be an Indian. Everybody was just behaving normally! Janna felt so disappointed she could hardly swallow.

Mr. Jenkins glanced at his watch. "Time to pack, School Kids!" he announced. "Head back to your cabins."

"School Kids," Micah muttered, as most of the students headed out of the Dining Hall. "I'd rather be a Camp Kid."

Janna didn't budge. "I can't pack without Slithers!" she exclaimed loudly.

Mr. Jenkins and Mrs. Grand stood side by side, gazing up at the buffalo. "Maybe I should lasso that snake," the teacher suggested.

Mrs. Grand grinned at him. "Perhaps we should move a table over to stand on . . . unless you're particularly good with a rope, cowboy."

Micah chewed on the end of his glasses. "Why doesn't someone just climb up?"

"That's impossible," Janna snapped.

"I guess so," Micah agreed doubtfully.

"Hah! I can do it!" David exclaimed. "I'm a squirrel, aren't I?"

Janna crossed her arms. "Don't be *ridiculous!*"

"I can climb anything!" David bragged. He clenched his hands into fists.

"Bet you can't!" Janna teased.

"Can, too!" David hopped up and down and gave her his best dirty look.

"I dare you!" Janna sang out. She loved it when David got this mad. Besides, he deserved it for making her so upset that she had dumped that canoe yesterday. "I double dare you!"

"Just watch!" David muttered furiously. He leaped at the stone wall of the fireplace and started climbing. Janna didn't believe how fast he moved. He seemed to be finding invisible footholds in the stones.

Mr. Jenkins stepped underneath him. "David, I suggest you come down here," he said in his too-calm voice that he used when children were doing something dangerous.

Yet David climbed with the speed of a squirrel.

A ridge of wood surrounded the buffalo like a picture frame on the wall. The bottom of that ridge was as high as the top of a door. David set the side of his foot on the ridge and stepped across the top of the fireplace toward Buffy.

Mrs. Grand gasped, clenching her cowgirl bandana in both hands.

David balanced on the edge of one foot. Then he threw one arm across the buffalo's broad forehead and leaned most of his weight on Buffy. His heels rested on the ridge behind him. "Told you I could do it," David crowed, and laughed triumphantly. "A squirrel can climb anywhere."

None of the students, or the adults, made a single sound. Janna stared up at David. A prickly feeling rushed up her spine and then back down again. Eliza-

beth moved to lean against Janna's shoulder. Micah stood behind them, next to his aunt. The room stayed completely silent.

David's expression of triumph slowly slipped from his face. His squirrel tail even drooped between his legs.

"You put Slithers up there!" Janna accused. "That means *you* came into Red Fox and stole my snake! Thief!"

David opened his mouth to answer, but no sound came out. It was the only time in all the years that Janna had known him that David was speechless.

Elizabeth pointed up at him, her arm stiff. "You spread the peanuts all over our porch to attract that raccoon to our cabin!"

David lowered his chin to rest on the buffalo's head. He clearly wished he could vanish.

Mr. Jenkins turned to face the two girls, astonished. "He did *what*?"

"And you put the frog in my sleeping bag last night!" Janna exclaimed, glaring at David and putting her hands on her hips.

The custodian and Mr. Jenkins stared at each other, their eyes wide, as if they were asking, *When did all this happen, without us noticing?* Then Mr. Jenkins gave David his fiercest teacher look.

The boy seemed to shrink in size.

"A frog in your sleeping bag?" Mr. Jenkins exclaimed, his voice cracking with surprise. "Janna, are you absolutely sure?"

"We're sure!" Janna and Elizabeth cried at the same moment. Janna stepped closer and pointed at David, too. "You, David Winesal, are the Camp Buffalo trickster!"

13
Home, Sweet Home

David sheepishly handed Slithers to Janna. "I only played all those tricks to tease you and the other girls."

Janna clutched Slithers in her arms. Slithers was very glad to see her. Janna wrapped the snake around her neck and gave her an extra big snakey hug.

Mrs. Grand tapped her foot as David climbed down from the buffalo. Then she said to him, "You'd better find a different way to let a girl know you like her, young man."

David's face turned from a chocolate brown to a deep purple.

Janna put her hands on both sides of her face and screamed. Howling, she ran all the way to her cabin. Janna raced into Red Fox with Elizabeth right behind her and announced that David had been the trickster all along. In fact, Janna stood in the middle of a circle of girls and told the whole story twice. She was just acting out her part of sneaking to the pond last night when Mrs. Grand walked through the doorway. "Packing?" the custodian asked.

Janna leaped toward her trunk and started stuffing in her pink rug. She didn't want Mrs. Grand to know about last night! The girls swept the dust out of the cabin. They carried their backpacks to the bus. With Slithers still wrapped around her neck, Janna dragged her trunk across camp. She wasn't going to let this wandering snake out of her sight.

After lunch, the third-graders marched onto the bus, singing "Michael, Row the

Boat Ashore." The same mustached driver started the vehicle with a roar, and the bus bumped down the dirt road.

Janna waved to Rainbow as Camp Buffalo disappeared in the distance. She had survived camp! She called, "Happy hopping, Tuffy. Bye, Coo. Be a rainbow, Silky!" Then Janna started singing another song at the top of her lungs, "Who took the cookies from the cookie jar?" Of course, most of the kids knew the words. The bus rattled and shook with the cheerful noise.

In the front seat, Mr. Jenkins leaned closer to David. The teacher had insisted that David sit with him so that they could have a chat. Janna wondered if the "chat" was similar to her mother's tea talks.

To her surprise, Janna discovered that she felt only a teensy bit mad at David. In fact, Janna had to admit that she wished she'd thought of playing the tricks herself. Both she and David liked teasing people, and his tricks had made camp lots more fun. Everyone had enjoyed seeing Slithers hanging from Buffy's neck. Besides, right now David looked as uncomfortable as a mouse being stalked by a cat.

Janna slipped into the seat behind Mr. Jenkins. She leaned closer. The other kids were making so much noise singing that she knew no one else could hear. Janna tapped Mr. Jenkins's shoulder. "You aren't going to call David's dad, are you?"

Mr. Jenkins just looked at her. Oops, she had forgotten. Their teacher never talked about one student's business with another. That was one of his class rules. So Janna rattled on, all in one breath, "Because, I wish you wouldn't call his dad. David didn't hurt anybody, not even the frog. He played the tricks on me, mostly. And I broke the rules *three* times, and you didn't call my parents! Besides, I'm willing to forgive him." Janna looked slyly out of the sides of her eyes at David. "Maybe."

David clutched his hands together and half turned toward Janna. "I'm sorry!" he moaned, and Janna could tell he truly meant it. Then David looked up at his teacher, begging, "Mr. Jenkins, my father will be so angry if you call him that he will hang me upside down by my toes in the basement all weekend!"

Mr. Jenkins raised his eyebrows.

"Well," David admitted more honestly, "he will take away my computer privileges for a week!"

Mr. Jenkins leaned back in his seat, his long legs stretched out into the aisle. "I was thinking of another possible consequence." He always said *consequence* rather than *punishment*.

"What?" David asked so eagerly that his voice shot up high. "I mean . . . what, Mr. Jenkins?" he added.

"You'll have to promise to do your best job on this project," Mr. Jenkins said. "And to be perfectly behaved in class for the next . . . let's say the next month."

"Oh, I promise, teacher!" David replied, beginning to bounce in his seat. "No more tricks."

"In that case," Mr. Jenkins said slowly, "since you have such a fascination with Slithers, I'd like you to write a ten-page story about our Storytelling Snake for the Camp Memory Board."

"Ten pages?" David exclaimed.

Janna gasped, too. But she knew David was the only one in the class capable of writing so much.

David stopped bouncing. "That will take me the whole weekend," he said.

Mr. Jenkins nodded. "I expect so. I want you to write the finest story you've ever written."

David swallowed and said in his most respectful voice. "I'll do my best work, sir."

Janna sat back, pleased. She could see the city in the distance out the bus window. Then they passed the new ten-screen movie theater. At the start of the next verse in the song, she sang, "David stole the cookies from the cookie jar!"

"Who me?" David cried cheerfully. "Couldn't be!"

The entire bus laughed.

David blushed. "Does *everybody* know what I did?" He leaned closer to Janna so she could hear him above the singing.

"Everybody," Janna said in her wickedest voice. "I made sure of that."

David groaned. Then he hissed, "What did you do with that frog last night?"

"Wouldn't you like to know," Janna replied, grinning. She was *never ever* going to tell him.

Before Janna knew it, the bus pulled into the parking lot at Martin Luther King Jr. Elementary. Every inch of the sidewalk and half of the lawn was filled with parents. Janna cheered. She could see her whole family by the picnic table.

Somehow she managed to be the third person off the bus. She raced forward and threw her arms around Mama. *I'm so glad to see you,* she said in Spanish, *"Me allegro mucho de verte."* And to think she'd once believed that her family drove her nuts. That seemed so long ago.

Dad looked surprised. "Are you all right, sweetheart?"

"I'm positively wonderful," Janna replied. She kissed her dad on the cheek.

Manuel hung back, as if afraid of interfering or being shoved away. Janna ruffled his hair. "Come here, squirt. Don't you want a hug?"

"Hermana!" Manuel cried happily, and launched himself at her. Janna twirled in a circle with her little brother in her arms. He was getting heavy. She'd been thinking during the last part of the bus ride of turning over a new leaf. She'd decided she wanted to become an absolutely perfect daughter and an A++ sister.

Janna laughed as she set Manuel down. She knew herself well enough to know that she'd get tired of being perfect in less than a week, maybe in less than ten minutes. She liked being mischievous too much! Still . . . Janna hugged Mama and her dad and Manuel again in a big *humongous* squeeze. She was sure glad they were all a family!